Samuel Alden Smith

Miscellaneous Assyrian Texts of the British Museum

with textual notes

Samuel Alden Smith

Miscellaneous Assyrian Texts of the British Museum
with textual notes

ISBN/EAN: 9783337235802

Printed in Europe, USA, Canada, Australia, Japan

Cover: Foto ©Andreas Hilbeck / pixelio.de

More available books at **www.hansebooks.com**

MISCELLANEOUS

ASSYRIAN TEXTS

OF THE

BRITISH MUSEUM,

WITH

TEXTUAL NOTES.

BY

SAMUEL ALDEN SMITH.

LEIPZIG:

EDWARD PFEIFFER.

———

1887.

TO MY HONOURED FRIEND AND FORMER CLASSMATE,

JOHN R. SAMPEY, D.D.,

WHOSE HIGH ATTAINMENTS IN THE STUDY OF

ORIENTAL LANGUAGES

HAVE SECURED FOR HIM A PROFESSORSHIP IN THE

"SOUTHERN BAPTIST THEOLOGICAL SEMINARY,"

LOUISVILLE, KY., U.S.A.,

THIS WORK IS AFFECTIONATELY DEDICATED.

PREFATORY REMARKS.

No one can deny the rapid advance that has been made in our knowledge of Assyrian during the last few years. The published texts have been carefully studied and many of the more important inscriptions have been translated and explained. Notwithstanding this the great part of the Assyrian literature which still remains wholly unknown to its most diligent students justifies without apology the publication of any new texts. Our knowledge of Assyrian is and must remain in a formative state until many more texts are published, studied and explained. No good Semitic scholar would maintain that any language could become well or thoroughly known so long as the text to a large section of its literature remains inedited. It is, therefore, much more important to devote time and study to a careful edition of new texts than to constantly direct the attention of scholars to the conclusive results to which we have arrived, or to strive to subject Semitic philology to the mandate of Assyrian. It is commendable to follow the example of the Continental School of Assyriologists in endeavouring to make our knowledge of the published inscriptions more exact, but it is very unwise to neglect the limits which our knowledge of Assyrian must necessarily have, until volumes of syllabaries, letters and contracts have been published.

The student of Assyrian may justly complain that the editions of texts are not critical enough. The editors too often do not take the trouble to compare the original as frequently as is necessary, especially in editing difficult texts. Such editions require much labor, patience and pains, which most Assyriologists seem unwilling or unable to devote to them. Many students able to remain in London but a few weeks (by no means long enough to acquire skill in copying the cuneiform characters) are induced to publish texts which they have not collated after copying them. Of course, under such circumstances, critical notes are an impossibility and mistakes are unavoidable. Absolutely faultless copies ought not, however, to be expected; for every one is aware how difficult it is to guard against mistakes in copying and printing plain English. The editor, therefore, does not claim that his edition is perfect, although he has carefully corrected the proof of each text from three to five times with the tablet, and used every care both here and in his *Asurbanipaltexte* to make his publications as reliable as possible.

Type is certainly preferable to any other form for such an edition of texts, but it often occasions great difficulty in exactly reproducing the characters. It has usually been possible to do this, otherwise a note will be found pointing out any defects. The editor has been very much aided by the printers, Messrs. Harrison & Sons, who have kindly cooperated with him in giving to the student as reliable a book as possible. He feels sure, therefore, that all who use the book will join him in this expression of thanks.

In the preparation of his work, *Die Keilschrifttexte Asurbanipals*, the author had occasion to copy inscriptions which could not be published in that book; these bilingual texts, incantations, syllabaries, etc., accompanied by others chosen especially for it, form the present work. The plan is to supplement this with other parts as soon as time and opportunity will permit.

The purpose of the accompanying critical notes is to give a reason for the reading that has been adopted, to indicate other possibilities, and to furnish here and there hints as to the probable translation and explanation; but they are intended to be in no sense a commentary.

Thanks are here due to Mr. T. G. Pinches, who has kindly read the final proof of most of the plates. Space is cheerfully given to him for three interesting texts which he prepared for publication some time ago.

SAMUEL ALDEN SMITH.

LONDON, *July 25th*, 1887.

5.

10.

15.

20.

25.

I

30.

35.

40.

45.

50.

2

55.

60.

65.

70.

75.

3

80. ⸢cuneiform signs⸣

85. ⸢cuneiform signs⸣

REV.

⸢cuneiform signs⸣

90. ⸢cuneiform signs⸣

95. ⸢cuneiform signs⸣

100. ⸢cuneiform signs⸣

105. ⸢cuneiform signs⸣

110. 𒀀 ⋯ ⋯

115. ⋯ ⋯

120. ⋯ ⋯

125. ⋯ ⋯

130. ⋯ ⋯

135. ⋯ ⋯

5.

10.

15.

20.

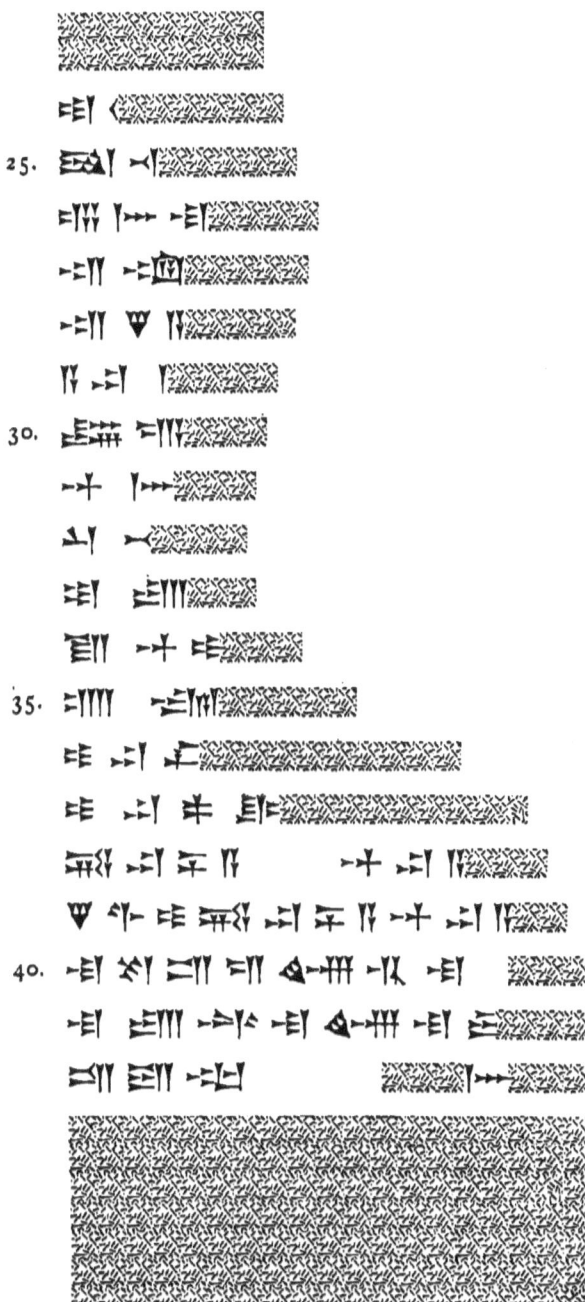

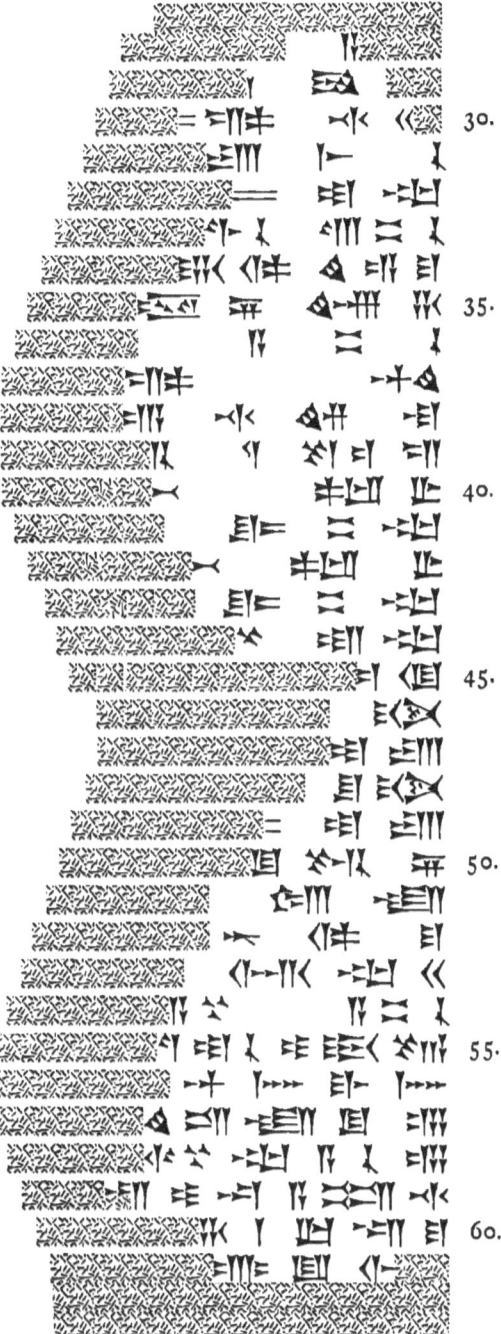

5.

10.

15.

20.

25.

5.

10.

15.

20.

REV.

25.

30.

35.

S. 48 + S. 799 + S. 1017 + S. 1347.

REV.

14

5.

10.

15.

REV.

20.

25.

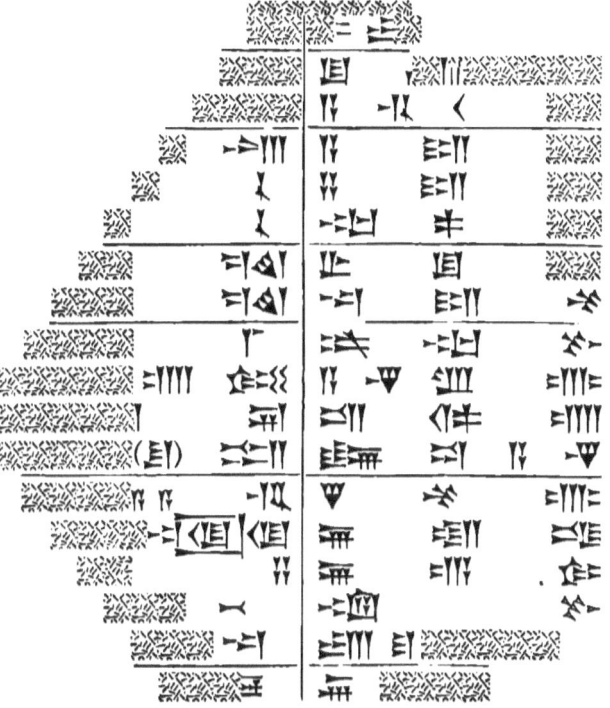

REV.

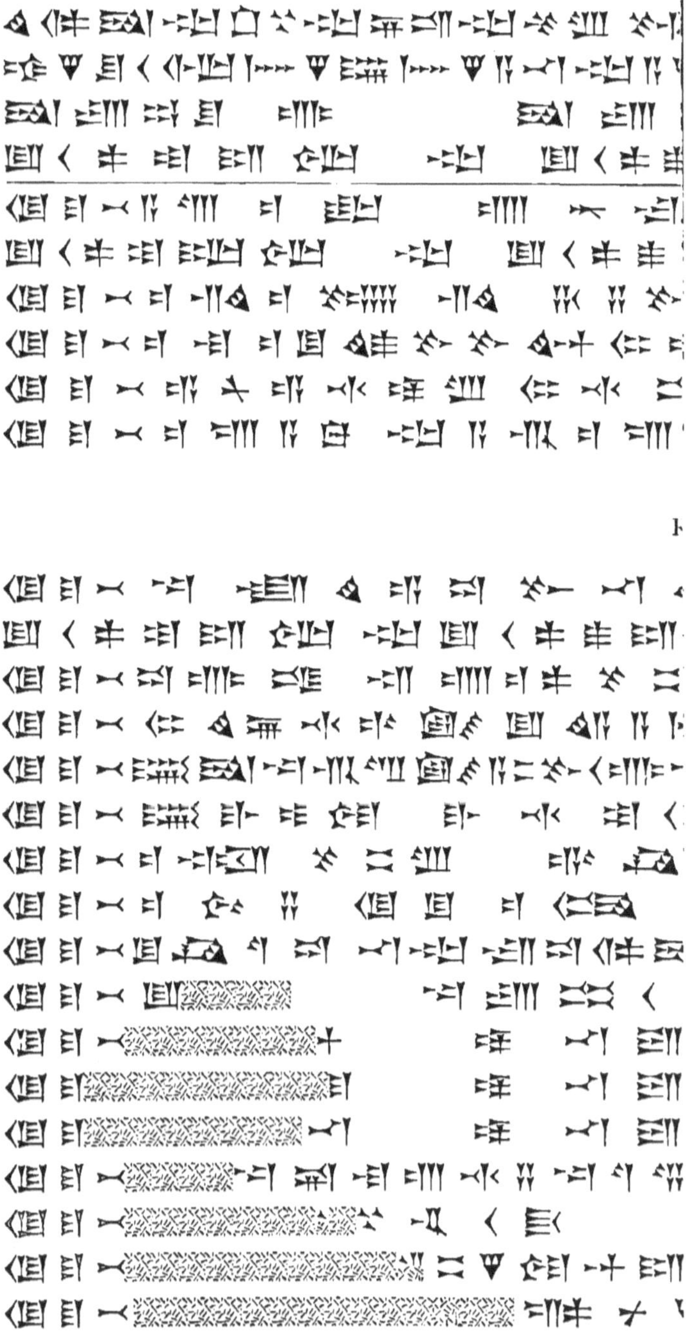

𒁹𒊹𒌋𒁹𒊹𒁹𒊹𒁹𒊹𒁹𒊹𒁹𒊹𒁹
𒁹𒊹𒌋𒁹𒊹𒁹𒊹𒁹𒊹𒁹𒊹𒁹𒊹𒁹
𒁹𒊹𒌋𒁹𒊹𒁹𒊹𒁹𒊹𒁹𒊹𒁹𒊹𒁹
𒁹𒊹𒌋𒁹𒊹𒁹𒊹𒁹𒊹𒁹𒊹𒁹𒊹𒁹

───────────────────────────────

𒁹𒊹𒌋𒁹𒊹𒁹𒊹𒁹𒊹𒁹𒊹𒁹𒊹𒁹
𒁹𒊹𒌋𒁹𒊹𒁹𒊹𒁹𒊹𒁹𒊹𒁹𒊹𒁹
𒁹𒊹𒌋𒁹𒊹𒁹𒊹𒁹𒊹𒁹𒊹𒁹𒊹𒁹 𒁹 𒁹 𒁹
𒁹𒊹𒌋𒁹𒊹𒁹𒊹𒁹𒊹𒁹𒊹𒁹𒊹𒁹 𒁹 𒁹 𒁹
𒁹𒊹𒌋𒁹𒊹𒁹𒊹𒁹𒊹𒁹𒊹𒁹𒊹𒁹 𒁹 𒁹 𒁹
𒁹𒊹𒌋𒁹𒊹𒁹𒊹𒁹𒊹𒁹𒊹𒁹𒊹𒁹 𒁹 𒁹 𒁹

𒁹𒊹𒌋𒁹𒊹𒁹𒊹𒁹𒊹𒁹𒊹𒁹𒊹𒁹
𒁹𒊹𒌋𒁹𒊹𒁹𒊹𒁹𒊹𒁹𒊹𒁹𒊹𒁹
𒁹𒊹𒌋𒁹𒊹𒁹𒊹𒁹𒊹𒁹𒊹𒁹𒊹𒁹 𒁹 𒁹 𒁹
𒁹𒊹𒌋𒁹𒊹𒁹𒊹𒁹𒊹𒁹𒊹𒁹𒊹𒁹 𒁹 𒁹 𒁹
𒁹𒊹𒌋𒁹𒊹𒁹𒊹𒁹𒊹𒁹𒊹𒁹𒊹𒁹 𒁹 𒁹 𒁹
𒁹𒊹𒌋𒁹𒊹𒁹𒊹𒁹𒊹𒁹𒊹𒁹𒊹𒁹 𒁹 𒁹 𒁹
𒁹𒊹𒌋𒁹𒊹𒁹𒊹𒁹𒊹𒁹𒊹𒁹𒊹𒁹 𒁹 𒁹 𒁹
𒁹𒊹𒌋𒁹𒊹𒁹𒊹𒁹𒊹𒁹𒊹𒁹𒊹𒁹 𒁹 𒁹 𒁹
𒁹𒊹𒌋𒁹𒊹𒁹𒊹𒁹𒊹𒁹𒊹𒁹𒊹𒁹 𒁹 𒁹 𒁹
𒁹𒊹𒌋𒁹𒊹𒁹𒊹𒁹𒊹𒁹𒊹𒁹𒊹𒁹 𒁹 𒁹 𒁹
𒁹𒊹𒌋𒁹𒊹𒁹𒊹𒁹𒊹𒁹𒊹𒁹𒊹𒁹 𒁹 𒁹 𒁹
𒁹𒊹𒌋𒁹𒊹𒁹𒊹𒁹𒊹𒁹𒊹𒁹𒊹𒁹 𒁹 𒁹 𒁹
𒁹𒊹𒌋𒁹𒊹𒁹𒊹𒁹𒊹𒁹𒊹𒁹𒊹𒁹 𒁹 𒁹 𒁹
𒁹𒊹𒌋𒁹𒊹𒁹𒊹𒁹𒊹𒁹𒊹𒁹𒊹𒁹 𒁹 𒁹 𒁹

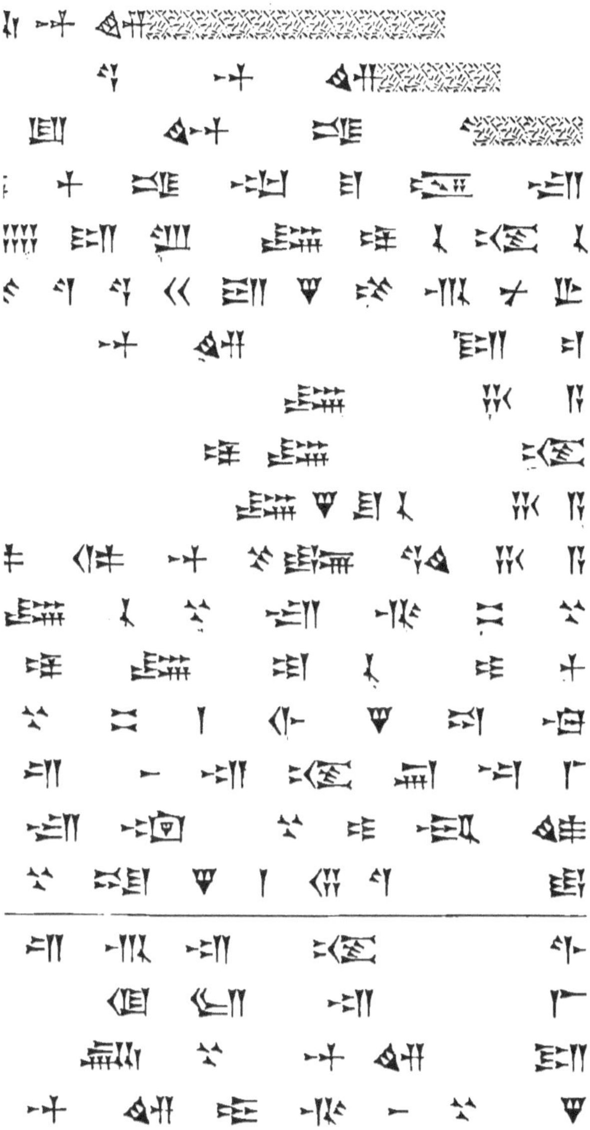

𒁹 𒀸 𒀭𒌋 𒌍𒉽𒋼𒍍 𒀸 𒐏 𒀸 𒀭𒌋
𒁹 𒀸 𒀭𒌋 𒌍𒉽𒋼𒍍 𒀸 𒐏 𒀸 𒀭𒌋

𒀭𒌋 𒌍𒉽 𒀭𒌋
𒁹 𒀸 𒀭𒌋 𒀸 𒀭𒌋 𒌍𒉽 𒀭𒌋 𒌍𒉽 𒍍
𒀸 𒅗 𒌍𒊺 𒌋𒄀 𒀸 𒈬𒌋𒌋 𒌍𒀭 𒌋𒅗
𒁹 𒀸 𒀭𒌋 𒀸 𒀭𒌋 𒌍𒉽 𒀭𒌋 𒌍𒀭 𒍍
𒁹 𒀸 𒀭𒌋 𒀸 𒀭𒌋 𒌍𒉽 𒀭𒌋 𒅗 𒍍
𒁹 𒀸 𒀭𒌋 𒀸 𒀭𒌋 𒌍𒉽 𒀭𒌋 𒌍𒊺 𒍍

𒌋 𒌍𒋼 𒁹𒊺 𒌍𒐊 𒌍𒄀 𒌍𒋼

𒁹 𒀸 𒀭𒌋 𒅗 𒀸 𒀸 𒌍𒍍 𒁹 𒐏 𒀸 𒀸 𒐈
𒌍𒐊 𒐈𒐈 𒌍𒉽 𒌍𒀭 𒁹 𒀸 𒀸 𒀸 𒌍𒐊
𒌋𒌍𒐊 𒌍𒐊 𒐈 𒌋𒌍 𒌍𒐊 𒌍𒐊
𒌍𒐊 𒀸 𒁹 𒀸 𒐊 𒐊 𒐊 𒍍 𒌍𒐊
𒌍𒐊 𒌍𒐊 𒌍𒍍 𒁹𒌋 𒌍𒐊 𒁹
𒌍𒐊 𒌍𒐊 𒌍𒐊 𒌍𒍍 𒌍𒐊 𒁹
𒌍𒐊 𒁹 𒌍𒐊 𒌍𒐊 𒌍𒍍 𒌍𒐊
𒌍𒐊 𒁹 𒀭 𒌍𒐊
𒌍𒐊 𒌍𒐊 𒌍𒐊
𒌍𒐊 𒌍𒐊

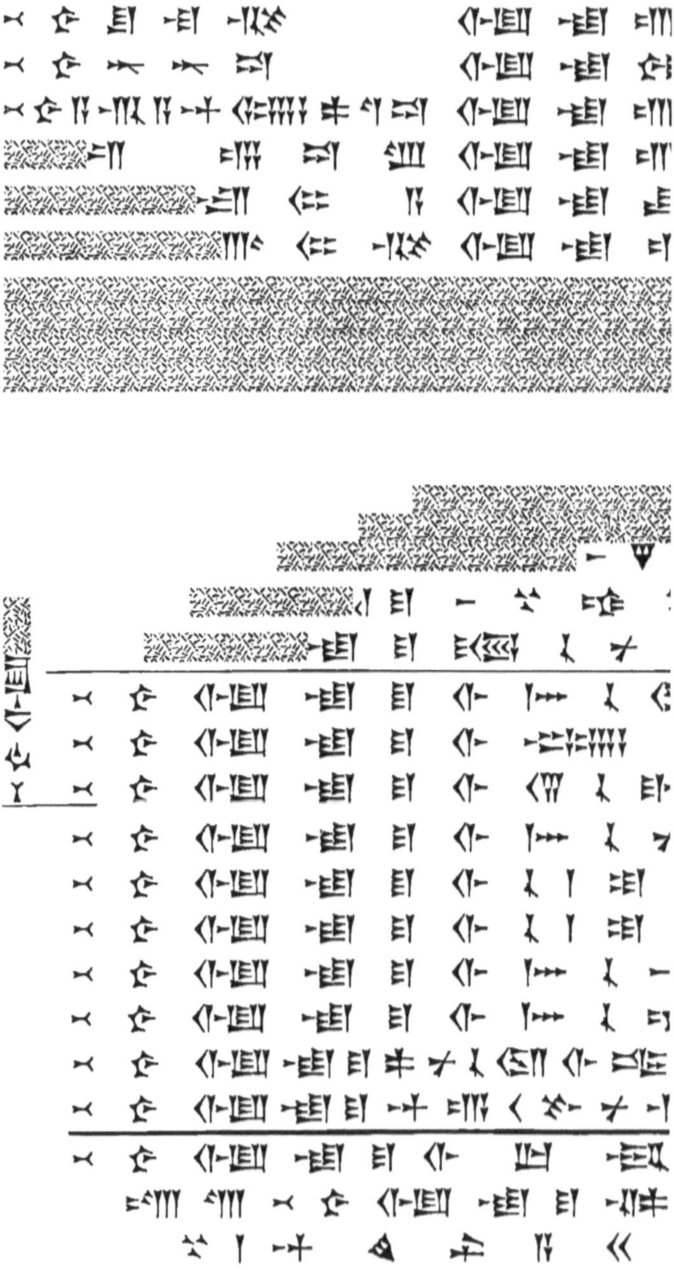

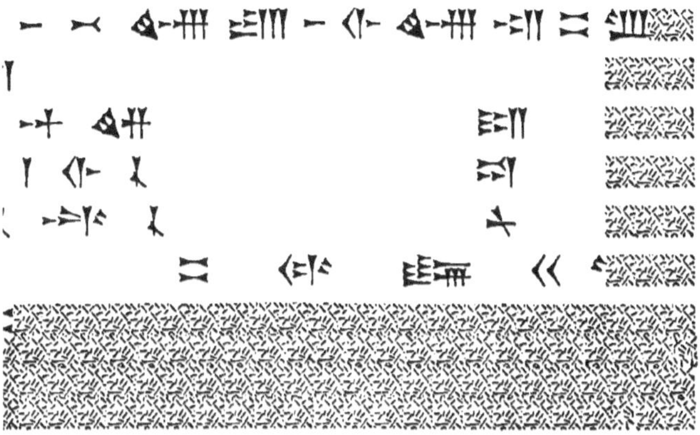

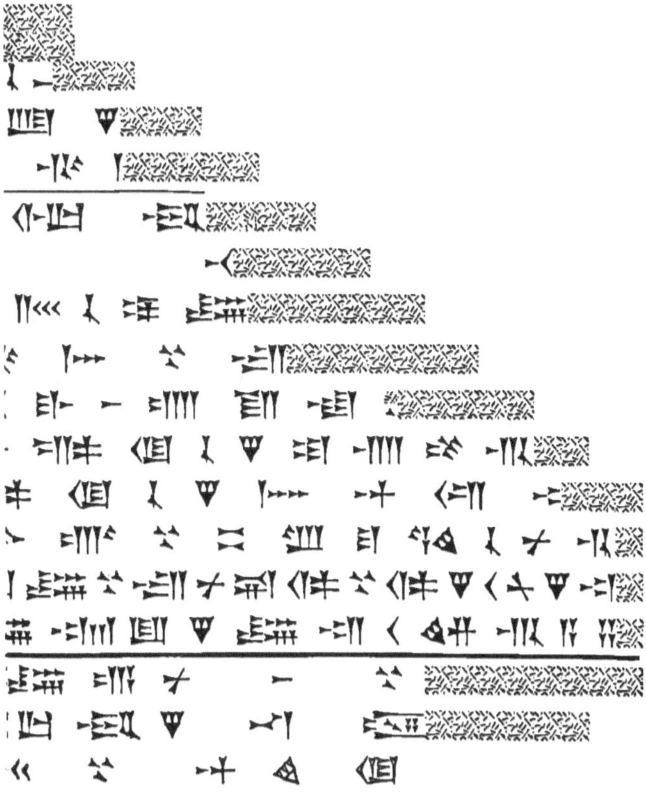

S. 526.

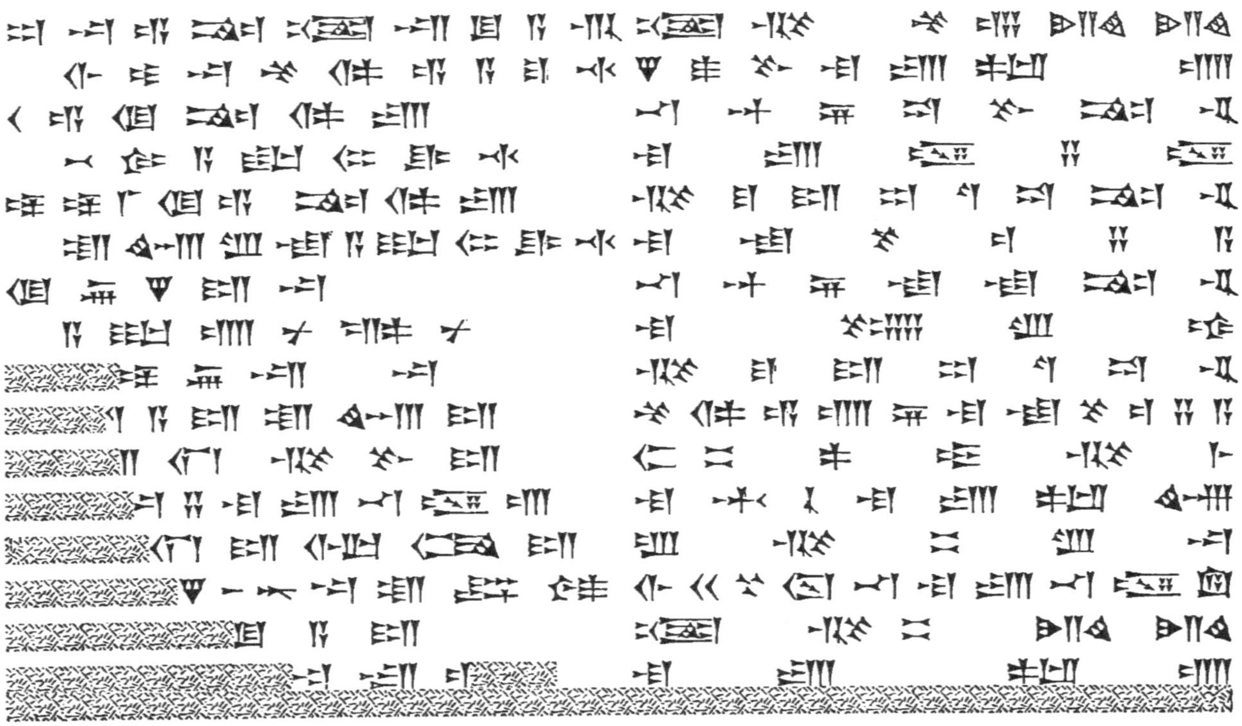

82-8-16, 1. O

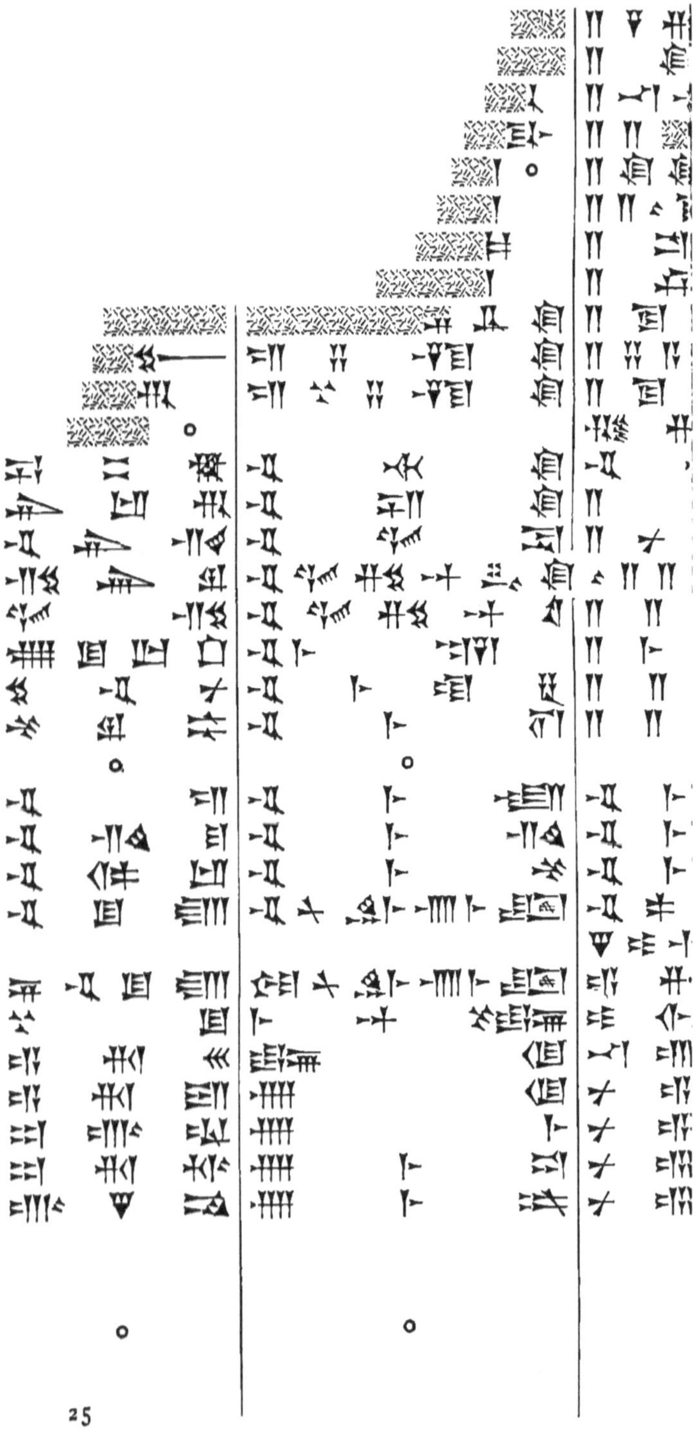

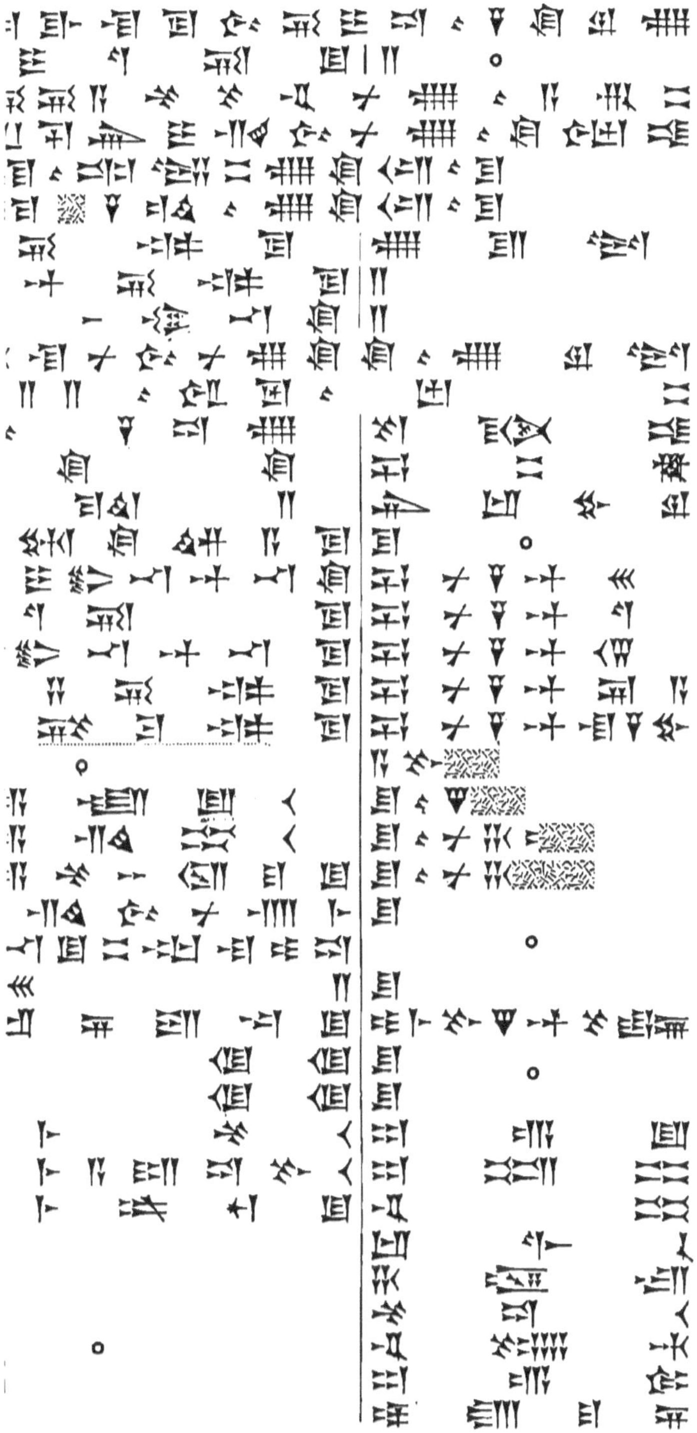

REVERSE.

LUMN IV).

76-11-17, 601.

3.

6.

9.

12.

15.

18.

REV.

21.

24.

27.

30.

33.

ON BOTTOM EDGE.

TEXTUAL NOTES.

———o———

K. 3473 + 79-7-8, 296 + Rm. 615.

These fragments, joined together by Mr. Pinches, form a part of the creation legend. This is unpublished, except that Delitzsch has given lines 17—42 in transcription in his *Assyrisches Wörterbuch*, p. 100. Although the text is very clear, he has made some mistakes which will be pointed out below.

Line 13. The first character is very probably correctly given, though it is not all to be seen.

Line 15. The first sign visible is apparently ⟨⊏.

Line 16. The first character is probably ⊶⊰⌐.

Line 23. Delitzsch completes the line [*ma*]. It is difficult to see why he should compare *ḫu-bur* with Homoroka, Omoroka?

Line 24. Delitzsch completes [*ḫê?*].

Line 25. The fourth sign has the value of *šin* and *šun*. At the end of the line there are traces which may be a part of ◁.

Line 26. Delitzsch completes [*li?*]

Line 27. The ⫶⫶⦉ is quite certain, notwithstanding the fracture in the tablet. Delitzsch completes the line [*ma?*]

Line 29. The fifth character is not ⊱⊨⊢⌐, as Delitzsch gives it, but quite clearly ⊨⊨⊢⌐. The difference between these two characters should be observed. *Cf.* Pinches *ZK* II, p. 158. The character preceding the last is not ⌐, as Delitzsch gives it, but is quite clearly ⊰⌐, which he queries in the margin.

Line 30. The fifth character is not ⊰⌐, as Delitzsch reads, but ⊰⌐. Delitzsch completes the line ⊬.

Line 32. Delitzsch completes ⊫⊨⌐⌐. This reading occurs in the next line.

Line 33. Delitzsch completes 𒂗.

Line 34. Perhaps the line is complete.

Line 37. There is the top-wedge ⪤ of a character visible, preceding *kun*, probably 𒂊.

Line 38. The last character visible is *rab*. Delitzsch gives incorrectly 𒂍.

Line 46. The beginning is not entirely complete, but the text seems to me to be correct.

Line 53. The last sign visible is probably ◁⟶.

Line 67. The last character that I have given is not quite certain, though highly probable.

Line 72. The last sign is of course ⊏.

Line 74. The last character is most probably *mis, lak*, as I have given it.

Line 75. The last part of what I have given is not clear. All the following lines of the obverse are much defaced. I am only able to read them by help of the same text which occurs above.

Line 90. *Cf.* line 32 above for the last sign.

Line 97. Not all the character *an* is visible.

Line 104. The tablet is broken here, but the text is clear l. 46 above.

Line 105. This line is lost at the beginning. *Cf.* line 47.

Line 112. The last sign is 𒂊, according to line 54 above.

Line 113. The character *kal* is not clear here, but *cf.* line 55 above.

Line 121. There are traces of the character preceding *u* ; what I see is 𒑲. Following *kur* there may be the same text as in line 63.

Line 125. The first sign is probably 𒂊.

Line 130. The first character is not clear, but it is quite certainly *an*.

Line 133. The last sign visible may be ⤙⪤.

Line 135. The eighth character is perhaps ⟶.

137. There are some traces of signs after *u* ; but I cannot recognise any further characters.

Line 138. This line is probably to be completed ⤙⪤.

K. 5640.

This small fragment is very imperfect. The occurrence of *ti-a-ma-at*, line 13, shows that it belongs to the creation story.

Line 2. The fourth character is not clear, but the text I have given is probably correct.

Line 4. The value of the first character is *utuk*, and that of the fourth *gidim;* these are names of demons.

Line 5. The last character is probably ⊢⊣⊺.

Line 6. The character ⊬ is not clear, but the sense seems to require it, and the traces are not against it. The last character is to be completed ⊢⊑⟨⟩.

Line 8. The character ⊒⊏ has the value of *ru*, and is to be read so here.—The ninth sign is possibly ⊨⊟⊞.

Line 10. There are some traces of wedges at the end of the line, but the signs are not to be recognised.

Line 14. The first character may be ⊨⊓, but seems to me to be more probably ⊨⊟⊺⊺⊺.

Line 15. The third and second signs from the end may be ⊨⊨⟨ ⊸⊺, and the last character is possibly ⊨⊺⊺.

Line 17. The last sign is probably ⊨⊟⊺⊺⊺.

Line 18. The second character may be ⊢⊨⊺.

Line 28. The second character is to be completed ⊣⊺⟨.

Line 32. The second sign is perhaps ⊣⊺⟨.

Line 35. The first character is perhaps better ⊨⊟⊺⊺⊺⊺.

Line 36. The third character is to be completed ⊿⊿.

Line 38. The ⊺⊻ at the end of this and the following line is quite certain, though not perfectly clear.

K. 4832.

Line 2. The first character is probably ◁⊢⊞.

Line 5. At the beginning there are traces of ⟨.

Line 12. The character before the last is perhaps ⟨⊺⊢.

Line 13. Perhaps the traces of signs preceding *pi* are to be completed ⊬ ⊨⊨ ⊢⊣⊺.

Line 14. The first character is, perhaps, ⊣⊣.

Line 20. The first sign is, perhaps, ⊬⊰ or ⊢⊺⊺⊰.

Line 25. The character at the beginning is, perhaps, ⸢𒅋⸣, though this is very doubtful.

Line 26. There are traces of other characters each side of the *an*, but I cannot tell what they are.

Line 29. The last character is probably 𒈫.

Line 30. The last sign is not very clear, but *šu* is, I am quite sure, correct.

Line 34. At the beginning of the line there are traces · of part of a character.

Line 39. The second sign may be 𒀭.

Line 52. The first character is not certain.

Line 53. At the beginning of the line there is part of a character to be seen, perhaps 𒈨.

Line 55. The 𒀭 at the beginning is probably part of 𒈠.

Line 57. The 𒀸 at the beginning is probably part of 𒈾. Part of the last upright wedge is visible.

Line 58. The sign at the beginning may be 𒆤, but is more probably 𒅋.

Line 59. At the beginning of the line the character is probably 𒊑, but it may possibly be 𒌋.

Line 60. The sign previous to the last seems to be *zu*, though it may be 𒊑; the word would then be *lik-ba*.

K. 3445.

This small fragment may be a part of the creation tablet just given. It was placed apparently by George Smith with these tablets in the case in the British Museum. The presence of the division marks and the style seem to indicate that it belongs to a legend of some kind. It is so fragmentary that I cannot determine with certainty where it really does belong.

In the first line visible, the second character is probably to be completed 𒅀. Further signs I am unable to restore from the traces that I can see.

Line 3. The sign *ki* at the end may not be entirely certain, but it is probably correct.

Line 8. Read *mi-iḫ-rit*. The *a-na-ku* at the end seems to me clear.

Line 9. The last character visible may be ⤩. The ⊢ is quite clear as I have given it.

Line 11. The two small wedges on the edge seem to me to be the division marks, though they may possibly belong to the following character, which is broken away.

Line 12. *zu-ab* is an ideograph for *apsû*, " abyss."

Line 13, *nu-bat-* (?) *ta*. This is perhaps the same word as the well-known *nubatte, nubatti*, "festival." It is, of course, altogether wrong to read ⤩ = *ul*, and to derive *mit-ti* from מות, as Dr. Lehmann, ZA II, p. 65, has done. The *is* after the *ta* is not clear, and may belong to the character that is partly broken away.

Line 14. The second character is, perhaps, ⤩. *Cf.* line 12. Instead of *pat-is-mi*, as I have given it, the reading may be ▨⤞ *ša-ma-mi*, though I think my text is much more probable. The last character visible is probably *up*.

Line 17. The first sign is not clear; it may be 𒂊, but if so, it is made very differently from the one above it. The line is very much crowded.

Line 18. The first character is, perhaps, ⊢⊨ᛁ. The seventh character from the end seems to me certainly *lu*, though I would have expected ⊩ᛁ, for the word *ib-na-a* is common and occurs in the next line.

Line 20. The sign preceding the last may be ⤞ instead of *kul*.

Line 21. The first character after the shading is probably ⊨ᛁᛁᛁ.

Line 23. The sign at the beginning may be ⊢⊨ᛁ.

Line 24. The third character is very doubtful; what is to be seen may be ⊬ᛁ⊰ or ⊰, and the beginning of another character.

Line 25. The second character is probably *du*, as I have given it. The three wedges to the right are probably to be completed ◁.

Line 27. The *du* that I have given as the third character is extremely doubtful. I cannot suggest an alternative reading.

Line 28. Instead of *te* it is possible to read ⊲ᛁ.

K. 3931.

This text is labelled "Incantation, Dialectic." According to Bezold's *Literaturgeschichte*, it has not been referred to or published. The writing is large, clear, and beautiful Assyrian.

Line 1. Just above the character *tuk* part of a wedge is visible.

Line 4. The *ra* is not altogether certain; the following sign is entirely illegible.

Line 5. The first sign seems to be *tum* as I have given it, but it is not all to be seen.

Line 35. The first character visible is probably ⌐𒌋𒌋𒌋; there are also some traces before this, but I am not certain what the sign is.

Line 39. The name *Aššûr* is quite certain; two upper wedges of the sign *mat* are visible.

K. 4041.

This is a small very legibly written fragment, but only a part of one side is preserved. It has not been mentioned in any publication.

Line 8. The last sign is not very clear, but my text seems correct.

Line 14. The traces at the beginning of this and the following line are very uncertain; I have given what I can see.

Line 20. The character at the beginning has traces of an upright wedge, and may be part of 𒄭, 𒄭 or 𒂊𒄭.

Line 25. The sign *lu* is not all visible, but is quite certain.

S. 48, &c.

This bilingual text is quoted by Strassmaier, AV p. 1008 (Bezold, *Literaturgeschichte*, p. 318), where he has given quite correctly the first two sections of the double column to the left on the reverse. This is, however, on the fragment numbered, S. 799. The pieces were fitted together by George Smith.

The traces of signs at right hand corner of the obverse may be parts of ⫟⧉ 𒐊𒐊.

The tablet is broken just at the division mark on the right (reverse), but the characters are all preserved except the last sign of line 4. The *kan* in line 3 also extended slightly over the line.

K. 93.

The label in the British Museum calls this text a list of "Babylonian families." There is no mention made of this in any publication so far as I am aware. Bezold omits it from his list.

The first two lines are probably complete.

Line 3. The sign at the end may be 𒌍.

Line 10. The wanting character may be ⟨𒌍 as Mr. Pinches suggests to me. *Cf.* Strassmaier, AV No. 727.

Line 15. The upright wedges for "two" are written over the sign *kur*.

Rm. 343.

This bilingual list has never been referred to according to Bezold, *Literaturgeschichte.*

In the first line, the second character is undoubtedly 𒌍𒐊.

Line 2. At the right the character is possibly 𒌍𒐊, or 𒌍𒐊.

The glosses have been placed in ( ), since it was impossible to make all the characters smaller in type. The first sign in line 14 does not represent the original correctly. The *ki* should be much smaller and be beneath the *kab* at the end of the line above. The *ki* on the outside seems to have been put here to show what is inside the preceding character.

Line 16. The sign *bu* is probably all that this line contained.

Above the first line in the left hand column on the reverse, some traces of wedges are visible, but I cannot make out the characters. Perhaps the two wedges are part of 𒀀𒀀.

In lines 4–6 the *tig* is the first sign of the left hand column. The shading is intended to belong to the next column.

K. 2866.

This tablet has been quoted by Strassmaier, AV in twelve passages (*cf.* Bezold, *Literaturgeschichte*, p. 291); it can hardly, however, be considered similar to V, R. 47, as Dr. Bezold will recognize upon seeing the whole tablet. It is very clearly and beautifully written, and will need little comment.

Line 4. The last character according to Strassmaier, AV No. 6261, is ⟶.

Line 10. The *an* at the end is wanting in Strassmaier's copy, No. 6953.

Line 11. The last sign visible is probably ⟨sign⟩. Strassmaier No. 6953, has incorrectly ⟨sign⟩.

Line 12. Strassmaier, No. 6241, adds ⟨sign⟩, shading it and ending the line.

Line 13. At the end Strassmaier doubtfully ⟨sign⟩.

Line 15. The last character is probably the god Bêl.

Line 16. The last sign visible is perhaps ⟶.

Line 17. The *še-da* after the shading is not entirely certain, but it is the most probable.

Line 18. After the shading the character *nin* is not certain.

Line 23. The character at the beginning may be *uš* or *du*, but it is impossible to determine with certainty. The reading *na-aḫ* for the third and fourth signs I regard as quite probable, though the tablet is broken.

Line 25. It is quite doubtful what stood at the beginning, perhaps ⟨sign⟩.

Rev. line 6. The line is probably to be transcribed: *aḫû rabi-i aḫâtu rabi-ti abû u ummu na-ṣa-rum u na-ka-ru.*

Line 7. The fifth sign is probably *paššuru*, "dish," though I do not regard the reading as certain. After *tig* the *zi* is doubtful. The scribe seems to have written them together.

Line 8. The 6th character is partly broken away, but cannot well be anything else than *za*.

Line 9. The sixth sign is probably correct, though the tablet is broken.

Line 10. The fifth character is very probably ⟨sign⟩.

Line 15 is perhaps to be completed ⸢cuneiform⸣ "male-servant and female-servant."

Line 19. There is enough of the *ḫi* visible to determine what it is; ⸢cuneiform⸣ is probably what is lost, and the character partly visible is probably ⸢cuneiform⸣.

Line 21. The third character from the end is not exactly reproduced, but it was difficult to give it exactly with type.

Line 22. The last word is evidently *nap-pa-ḫa-tu*, "black-smithery."

Line 26—27. *Cf.* W.A.I., IV., pl. 7, Col. II, lines 2, 3, etc.; Pl. 8, Col. III, lines 3—5, etc.

Line 29. The line is probably to be completed ⸢cuneiform⸣ as Strassmaier, No. 7638, does.

K. 2169.

This omen-tablet is altogether unpublished. It has been quoted by George Smith in *Sennacherib*, p. 1, and *Assyrian Eponym Canon*, p. 173. *Cf.* Bezold, *Literaturgeschichte*, p. 286. The label on the box is "Omens from the wind, &c. Interesting writing of name of Sennacherib."

Line 1. The last sign visible is quite certainly *bul*.

Line 2. The marks above and below *tab* I regard as accidental.

Line 4. The third character before the last one given in my copy is not exactly reproduced; the middle horizontal wedge should pass through the upright ones.

Line 7. The character at the end of the line may be ⸢cuneiform⸣.

Line 14. For *an-še-te* see W.A.I., IV, 16. The correct reading is *ni-sa-ba*. For the value of *šum-ir* in Accadian, *cf.* Pinches, P.S.B.A., April, 1881, p. 83.

Rev. line 1. This seems to be the correct reading of what is to be seen here; the last *in* is not all visible.

Line 2. There are traces of several characters at the end, but I found it impossible to reproduce them; therefore I have given only some wedges to indicate that the text is not all broken away.

Line 10 is, perhaps, to be transcribed and translated thus: *u-ra-bi dim ab-šar ba-an-e,* "Like its old copy written and explained (shown forth)." *ba-an* are prefixes, and *e* the root (Pinches).

Line 11 *ff.* George Smith translates: "Tablet of Aia-suzubu-ilih, the scribe of the rabshakeh, of Sennacherib, the great royal son of Sargon, king of Assyria" (*Eponym Canon,* p. 173). The word *a-ba,* which Smith translates "scribe," is very difficult. *Cf. Asurbanipaltexte, Heft II,* p. 32. Delitzsch, in his *Wörterbuch,* accepts the meaning "Secretär," but it does not fit in many passages. Strassmaier proposes "Verwalter." We do not know how the Assyrians pronounced the group; it is, however, quite certain that *a-ba* is not "gut-semitisch," as Delitzsch claims. Line 14 below we have *a-ba amelu bel-bat-ki* (= *Aššûr*).

K. 258.

This tablet has never been mentioned in the published literature; it is entirely new. The writing is very clear, so that there is comparatively little to note. As will be seen, it is an "omentext."

Line 1. The character *ki* following the shading is very doubtful; what is visible may belong to two different characters.

Line 2. The eleventh character is possibly to be completed ⚹.

After line 11 the scribe has erased an entire line.

Line 12. At the end of the line, there are traces of a character that are possibly ⫣.

Line 14. The traces of signs visible before the shading are probably *an,* with the beginning wedges of the name of the god.

After line 15, the scribe has erased two lines. The tablet is broken away except in the middle, as I have indicated by the shading.

Line 16. I see some traces of signs in this line, just above the *li* of the following line, but they are not clear enough to enable me to reproduce them.

Line 17. The characters *si-li-ti* are clearly a gloss. At the end there are some traces, possibly two upright wedges.

Line 18. The third line is reproduced in print just as the scribe wrote it.

Line 23, is probably complete.

Line 24. The traces at the end of the line are, perhaps, to be completed ⊣𝟙.

Line 28. At the close of the line, the traces may be the beginning of ⊢𝖟⊣𝖞.

Line 29. I think this line is complete.

Line 32. The first sign is probably ⊢≻𝖞.

Line 34. The first character may be ⊑𝖞𝖞◂.

Rev. line 6. After this line, the scribe had left out a line and inserted it on the edge, and indicated where it belonged by a line. I have reproduced this in my copy.

Line 8. The wedge at the end is, perhaps, the lower wedge of 𝖞.

Line 10. The last character is probably to be completed ⊢𝖟⊣𝖞.

The last line is separated from the others, as is indicated, and is written in the style of writing that is found on the stones. It was evidently cut in after the tablet was baked. I think the line is complete as I have restored it.

S. 526.

This bilingual text has been cited several times. *Cf.* Bezold, *Literaturgeschichte*. There is no indication that the explanation " Weisheitsregeln und Sprüche (?) enthaltend (Delitzsch) " is correct. The text is clearly an address to a god, for line 15 we read, *be-lum a-na bît ši-ka-ri la tir-ru-ub*, " O God, into the house of drink thou dost not enter." *Cf.* lines 19, 23, &c. The entire reverse of the tablet is broken away.

Line 1. The character preceding *an* may be ⊑𝖞𝖞𝖞.

Line 2. The text here is restored according to the traces and from line 4 below.

Line 4. The upright wedge at the beginning is probably part of ⊨𝖞.

Line 9. The second character is probably ⊨𝖞𝖞.

Line 10. The recurrence of *a-ḫi-na* in the next line shows that ⊢ ⊢ is repeated here. *Cf.* line 6 above.

Line 11. Following *ṣi* there was probably 𒂊𒌋 𒊏 𒂍 𒊏 𒀀 𒌋.

Line 12. The sign with the shading seems to me to be 𒌋.

Line 17. The wanting character is most likely 𒄑.

Line 19. *Ši-tul-ti*. *Cf.* W.A.I., V, 16, line 1. The restorations are from line 15 above.

Line 20. I have restored from line 16.

Line 21. The last sign is *bit*, according to the last line on the tablet.

Line 26. I see traces of the corner-wedge of *ki*.

Line 27. Although the tablet is broken at the beginning, there is nothing lost.

Line 30. For the second sign visible, compare W.A.I., V, 38, line 8; II, 21, line 42 *cd*. The same character occurs at the beginning of line 32.

Line 35. The third character is probably 𒄑, followed by 𒄿 as in line 17 above.

82-8-16, 1.

This text, which is the only one bearing the above signature, is the bottom left hand corner of a large tablet, the probable original length of which was about 8 or 9 inches, and the width about 7 inches. The present length is 4½ inches, and the width 4 inches. Each side originally contained two fourfold columns, of which we have the lower part of the first, a few characters of the lower part of the second, a few characters of the upper part of the third, and the upper part of the fourth.

The first 20 lines of the first column, having been completed from an unbaked tablet from Babylon (Sp. II, 266), are given in the Babylonian style, the characters wanting on the Babylonian copy having been restored, transcribed into Babylonian, in order to prevent confusion by mixing the two styles. The readings of the Assyrian copy are given in the notes. After line 20 (the eighth line of the obverse of 82-8-

16, 1) the text is given according to the Assyrian copy. This tablet is mentioned by Bezold in his *Literaturgeschichte*, p. 350.

OBVERSE (COL. I).

Line 1. The sixth character, ⟨cuneiform⟩, is doubtful. The character ⟨cuneiform⟩ at the end of this line is broken in the original.

Line 3. The broken character at the beginning of this line is to be completed as ⟨cuneiform⟩.

Line 4. Before ⟨cuneiform⟩ are traces of a character which may be ⟨cuneiform⟩. The character after the second ⟨cuneiform⟩ may be ⟨cuneiform⟩.

Line 5. The fifth character of the third division (*šu*) is doubtful. The character *lam* (towards the end) is also uncertain—it may be simply ⟨cuneiform⟩ and ⟨cuneiform⟩ written over another character.

Line 6. The seventh character is uncertain, but the traces indicate *su* or *la* (*malašam*). As in the line above, the character *lam* is doubtful.

Line 7. The first character visible is to be completed as ⟨cuneiform⟩.

Line 9. The sixth character of the third division (*na*) is not clear in the original.

Lines 10 and 11. The first character of the second division is doubtful. The character *si* seems to be written differently.

Line 12. The characters *te* and *lil* are doubtful.

Line 13. The character *iḫ* of *Ebiḫ* is, in both cases, written more in the Assyrian than the Babylonian style. 82–8–16, 1, which begins with this line, has ⟨cuneiform⟩ in the first division.

Line 14. 82–8–16, 1 (the Assyrian text), has here ⟨cuneiform⟩ | ⟨cuneiform⟩ | ⟨cuneiform⟩.

Line 15. The Assyrian text has here ⟨cuneiform⟩ | ⟨cuneiform⟩ | ⟨cuneiform⟩, followed by traces of *us*.

Line 16. The Assyrian text has here ⟨cuneiform⟩ | ⟨cuneiform⟩ | ⟨cuneiform⟩.

Line 17. The Assyrian text has ⟨cuneiform⟩ | ⟨cuneiform⟩ | ⟨cuneiform⟩.

Line 18. The Assyrian text has ⟨cuneiform⟩ | ⟨cuneiform⟩ | ⟨cuneiform⟩.

Line 19. The Assyrian tablet has [cuneiform signs]

Line 20. The Assyrian text has [cuneiform signs]. The last three characters (*la-ša-bu*) are rather doubtful.

Lines 46–48. The ends of these lines are completed from the fragment Rm. 905.

[Of column 2 there are the beginnings of five lines, as follows: 1. [cuneiform], 2. [cuneiform], 3. [cuneiform], 4. [cuneiform], 5. [cuneiform]. Of the first column of the reverse (Col. III), are also the remains of five lines: 1. [cuneiform], 2. [cuneiform] (blank space for one line), 3. [cuneiform] (blank space for two lines), 4. [cuneiform], 5. [cuneiform], followed by traces of the first character of a sixth.]

REVERSE (COL. IV).

Line 26. The traces of the last character of this line which are to be seen may be part of [cuneiform], [cuneiform], or [cuneiform].

Lines 27 and 28. The traces of the last character in each of these two lines lend themselves to [cuneiform].

Line 29. The traces of characters in this line point to some such restoration as [cuneiform] (??)

T. G. P.

76–11–17, 601.

This text is inscribed on a small rectangular tablet of clay 2¼in. by 1⅞in. The writing is a good and fairly clear Babylonian hand, though the tablet has suffered slightly in some places. The text refers to a loan from Iddin-Marduk to Mušêzib-Marduk, and is dated in the 33rd year of Nebuchadnezzar. A *précis* of the contents has been given by me in the *Guide to the Nimroud Central Saloon*, p. 87, No. 31.

Line 1. The number at the beginning is broken away. The *ma* which follows is mutilated, and not very carefully written, as the wedges seem to be four in number, and of unequal length. The probability is, however, that the wedges of the number with which the text began crossed over as far as the upright of the *ma*, and that we are to read [cuneiform] or [cuneiform]. In *ina êštin šikli*, the ⊢ crosses the Ⲓ; and the same also takes place in the next line.

Line 4. In the last character (*nappaḫu*, "smith"), the scribe seems, judging from the traces, to have wavered between 𒂍𒄲 and 𒂍𒄲.

Line 10. The last character of this line (*ḫarrana*, "double road"="partnership") has the two upright wedges lightly impressed at the top of the character, close to the slanting wedges. The first character (*ki*) has four wedges within on the tablet.

Line 12. The character *zēr* at the end is doubtful, and *mu* is restored.

Line 13. The last character but one (*šu*) is doubtful, but the traces do not lend themselves well to anything else. The name is probably to be read *Nabû-bânu-šûtur*. For *bânu*, see W.A.I. II, pl. 36, l. 50 *cd*.

Lines 15—17. The *ki* in these lines also have four wedges within. (See line 10.)

Line 17. There is no upright wedge before the name Nebuchadnezzar.

At the end is room for two lines more in the original.

T. G. P.

K. 433.

This text is written on a tablet of baked clay, of a yellowish colour, 3¼ in. long by 2⅓ in, broad. Though marked with the letter "K," this tablet can not have come from Kouyunjik, as both the writing and the form of the text, which is dated at Erech, are Babylonian. The inscription is very clearly written, but has some peculiarities as to style. It is of great interest also on account of its being dated in the 20th year of Assurbanipal. A *précis* of the contents of the inscription has been given by me in the *Guide to the Nimroud Central Saloon*, p. 83, No. 23.

Line 1. The peculiar form of the character *šun* (the last character but three) is noteworthy.

Line 2. The character *aḫ* (the sixth ch.) has four upright wedges in the original. The character *ki*, in this text, varies slightly in form, the 3 horizontal sometimes only touching, and sometimes crossing the first upright wedge. The upper corner-wedge is sometimes in front of, and sometimes over, the character.

Line 6. The last character of this line has the small upright wedge written rather higher than here printed. The slanting wedges also are longer and not so much inclined.

Line 8. The second *ki* is rather roughly written in the original, and has 4 horizontal wedges within.

Line 10. The second character is doubtful; it is probably intended for ⩜.

Line 17. The character *sa* at the end has, in the original, the upper horizontal wedge longer than the lower one, and also a little more to the left.

Line 18. The upright wedge before 𐎺 was probably written after the scribe had finished the line, and may have been intended to be added to the 𐎨, so as to correct it to 𐎹.

Line 24. The last character but one, which is written in the original very much as here printed, probably has two upright wedges within, being apparently intended for the Babylonian form of ⫶⫶—very faint traces of a second wedge may, indeed, be detected.

Line 28. The last character but one has, in the original, the horizontal wedge very much to the right.

Line 29. The name of the god *Bêl* is written in a rather peculiar manner in the original, the slanting wedges being, in one case, almost vertical.

Line 30. In the original there is a false wedge before the character *mu.* Apparently the scribe had begun to write that character too close to the 𐎡.

Line 32. The character 𐎡 at the end is very roughly formed. The last sign but two (*ṣu*) has four horizontal wedges, and is crossed by one upright wedge, as in the Assyrian form.

Line 33. This line seems to have been inserted by the scribe after having completed the writing of the text, the characters being only a little more than half the size of those of the other lines.

Line 35 (bottom edge). The character ⸺ before 𐎨 is mutilated in the original, and therefore doubtful.

T. G. P.

HARRISON AND SONS, PRINTERS IN ORDINARY TO HER MAJESTY, ST. MARTIN'S LANE, LONDON.